Larry Bird

Bob Italia

Published by Abdo & Daughters, 6535 Cecilia Circle, Edina, Minnesota 55439.

Library bound edition distributed by Rockbottom Books, Pentagon Tower, P.O. Box 36036, Minneapolis, Minnesota 55435.

Printed in the United States.

Cover Photo: Allsport Photography USA, Inc.
Inside Photos: Allsport Photography USA, Inc.: 4, 17, 21, 24, 28, 30.
                FPG International: 13, 15.

Edited by Rosemary Wallner

Library of Congress Cataloging-in-Publication Data

Italia, Robert, 1955-
      Larry Bird / written by Bob Italia ; [edited by Rosemary Wallner].
          p. cm. -- (M.V.P. , most valuable player)
Summary: Examines the personal life and basketball career of the noted Boston Celtics player.

ISBN: 1-56239-122-4 (lib. bdg.)

1. Bird, Larry, 1956- --Juvenile literature. 2. Basketball players--United States--Biography--Juvenile literature. 3. Boston Celtics (Basketball team)--Juvenile literature. [Bird, Larry, 1956- . 2. Basketball players.] I. Wallner, Rosemary, 1964- . II. Title. III. Series: Italia, Robert, 1955-   M.V.P., most valuable player.
GV884.B57I83   1992
796.323 '092--dc20
[B]   92-20131
                                                         CIP
                                                         AC

Contents

Larry Bird's many basketball skills have made him
one of the best players of all time.

An All-Around Basketball Player

He can't jump, he can't run—but, boy, can he play basketball. Since joining the Boston Celtics in 1979, Larry Bird has been the Most Valuable Player (MVP) of the National Basketball Association (NBA) three consecutive years. He has led the Celtics to three NBA championships.

Not only is he an accurate shooter and a high scorer, Bird has excellent passing and rebounding skills. Throughout his career, he has been one of the league's most feared three-point shooters. When the game is on the line, Bird usually takes the final shot. His last-second heroics have become legendary. Combine these skills and qualities into a 6-foot 9-inch, 220-pound frame and you have one of the most gifted, all-around athletes ever to play in the NBA.

Growing Up in French Lick

Larry Joe Bird was born in the small rural town of West Baden Springs, Indiana, on December 7, 1956. He was the fourth child in a family of six. His parents, Joe and Georgia, were poor and always struggled.

Bird recalled how his house's old furnace would often break down, filling the house with smoke. Bird and his family would stand outside in the freezing weather while Bird's father tried to fix it. Usually by morning, the furnace was running again.

Joe Bird worked as a finisher at the nearby Kimball Piano & Organ Co. Joe was a hard worker but never seemed to make enough money. His creditors were always after him.

"I always hear he was the kind of guy who would give you the shirt off his back," Bird recalled. "A lot of people tell me them things now because of who I am. But I know the ones who're tellin' the truth."

Georgia was a waitress. She worked hard and did everything she could for her family.

"I remember, she worked a hundred hours a week and made a hundred dollars," Bird recalled, "and then went to the store and had to buy $120 worth of food. If there was a payment to the bank due, and we needed shoes, she'd get the shoes, and then deal with them guys at the bank.

I don't mean she wouldn't pay the bank, but the children always came first."

When things got too tough, Bird and his brother and sisters moved in with his grandmother, Lizzie Kerns. But Kerns wasn't much better off. She didn't even have a telephone.

Bird liked to fish for bluegills and hunt for mushrooms under elm trees. He also liked to play basketball.

Bird attended Springs Valley High School in French Lick, Indiana. There, Bird's passion for basketball blossomed. In his freshman year, Bird was just over six feet tall and a scrawny 135 pounds. Though his father didn't practice with Larry, he did offer his son a $20 reward if he made the freshman team. Inspired by the offer, Bird practiced hard— and won the $20.

On Sundays, he drove with friends to some larger town that had a Kentucky Fried Chicken franchise. Bird and his friends would buy a big bucket, then return to Springs Valley and play basketball all day.

Bird played many pickup games against older and taller kids. To survive on the court, Bird learned to fake and to shoot falling away. He also learned to dribble with both hands, and developed a long-range shot.

"You've got to understand," he said. "My whole life's been basketball. It was never a recreation for me. It was something I fell in love with."

But Bird never thought he would play professional basketball. "My goal in life when I was younger was to get out of school, work construction—be a construction guy and pour concrete," he said. "I never worried about what I would do, because I always knew I could do something. I put up hay all my life.

"In school," he added, "the only thing I thought about was basketball. But I went to class and did my homework. I felt sorry for players who didn't. I tried to talk to them because I knew they were going to have a tough life. And sooner or later it's the same thing on the basketball court. The guy who won't do his homework misses the free throw at the end.

"In high school we used to shoot fouls at 6:30 in the morning before class," he continued. "But one of my best friends never showed up. In the regional finals our senior year, he missed three one-on-ones in a row, and we lost in overtime. I never said nothing to him. I just looked at him and he knew."

Larry Bird was shy in high school. He hated crowds and rarely dated. He wouldn't watch his older brother Mark play basketball until his final varsity game. Avoiding crowds was a family trait. "My father was proud of us," said Bird, "but he wouldn't go see us play. Dad didn't like crowds either."

Bird's father had a drinking problem, which made it difficult for Bird to look up to him. Still, Bird learned some important lessons from his father.

"I remember one time," Bird said. "I was 13, or 14 maybe, and my father came home with an ankle all black and blue and red. He needed me and my brother just to get his boot off, and he was in awful pain. But the next morning we got the boot back on, and he went to work. That really made an impression on me."

Making His Way to Indiana State

Eighteen-year-old Larry Bird was the top senior high school scorer in Indiana. He averaged 30 points and 17 rebounds per game.

After high school, Bird went to Indiana University in Bloomington to play for their famous coach, Bobby Knight. But Bird was overwhelmed by Indiana's huge campus. He felt self-conscious about his background and clothing. Even more, he had little money and was lonely.

A month later, before preseason practice had begun, Bird quit and returned to French Lick. But his return was unpleasant and he became an outcast. His hometown fans felt he had embarrassed the town.

Bird found a maintenance job. Occasionally, he worked on garbage trucks. Though it wasn't glamorous, the job made Bird happy.

"I loved that job," he recalled. "It was outdoors and you were around your friends. I felt like I was really accomplishing something. How many times are you riding around your town and you say to yourself, 'Why don't they fix that? Why don't they clean the streets up?' And here I had the chance to do that. I had the chance to make my community look better."

Within the year, things got worse. His parents divorced. Then, dogged by creditors and his drinking problem, his father committed suicide.

Bird struggled with the tragedy. He felt lost. Then one day he talked to one of his father's friends. His name was Shorty. He owned a pool hall.

Shorty told Bird how his father had been a terrific basketball player. He might have become a professional. But he left school after the eighth grade and began to work. He never realized his dream.

Bird knew he had to leave French Lick if he wanted to make something of himself. Indiana State University in Terre Haute had tried to recruit Bird for their basketball team. Bird decided to enroll. But just when his life was getting back together, Bird rushed into a bad marriage in 1975. Within the year, he got a divorce. Then he discovered his ex-wife was pregnant.

Bird's daughter, Corrie, was born in August 1977. Bird, now in his junior year, wasn't allowed to spend much time with his daughter.

"When I was a kid, I thought people who got divorced were the devil," he recalled. "And then I go out and do it myself right away. Getting married was the worst mistake I ever made. Everything that ever happened to me, I've learned from it. But I'm still scarred by that. That scarred me for life. That and being broke are the two things that influenced me the most—still."

Bird probably wouldn't have survived that troubled period in his life if it hadn't been for his girlfriend Dinah Mattingly. He also gave credit to her for helping improve his basketball skills.

"Dinah was with me through all that stuff," he said. "She was there. I don't know how many times that poor girl stood under the basket and passed the ball back to me. Over and over, standing there, throwing it back to me so I could shoot. And then all the time takin' care of my injuries."

(Larry and Dinah eventually got married. Bird built a house in French Lick with a regulation basketball court and a satellite dish. Bird also bought a Ford-Lincoln-Mercury car dealership in nearby Martinsville.)

In 1978, Larry Bird found himself in the draft. Bird, now 6 feet 9 inches tall and weighing 220 pounds, had no intentions of skipping his senior year to play professional basketball. It didn't mean that much to him. He liked his life at Indiana State.

Besides, all his life he had heard that he was too slow, he couldn't jump, he couldn't run. He had gotten to a point where he believed it. So he didn't think of playing in the NBA.

Bird was on the golf course when he found out the Boston Celtics made him their No. 1 pick, sixth overall. He didn't even know what it meant. And he didn't know of the Celtics' rich basketball tradition. To him, they were just another team.

Bird stayed in school and had his best year ever. He was named the 1978-79 College Player of the Year. He averaged over 30 points a game and led the Indiana State Sycamores to 33 straight wins. In the national championship game against the Michigan State Spartans and Magic Johnson, Bird scored only 19 points. The Spartans won 75-64.

Just like that, Bird's college basketball career was over. Now he was the property of the Boston Celtics. But more importantly, Bird got his diploma—the first person in his family to do so.

Bird Becomes a Celtic

Bird signed for $650,000 a year, the best contract ever paid a rookie at the time. As a result, Celtic fans expected much from Bird. The once-proud Celtics had just finished a dismal season, winning only 29 games. Many hoped Bird would save their team.

When he signed with the Boston Celtics,
Bird became the highest paid rookie ever.

That was a lot of pressure to place on a young rookie's shoulders. But Bird, now 23 years old, responded like a champion that 1979-80 season. He was selected to play in the All-Star game, and led the Celtics to an amazing 61-21 record. It was good for first place in the tough Atlantic Division of the Eastern Conference.

Bird led the Celtics in scoring (21.3 per game), rebounds (10.4 per game), and steals. And he was named the NBA Rookie of the Year. Though the Philadelphia 76ers eliminated the Celtics from the play-offs, Bird led the Celtics in post season scoring with a 21.3 average. Fans knew that Larry Bird would one day lead the Celtics to a championship.

The 1980-81 season was filled with high expectations for Bird and the Celtics. They started slowly, but then Larry Bird took charge as they fought the 76ers for the top spot in the division. The Celtics beat Philadelphia on the last day of the season. Though both teams finished with 62-20 records, the Celtics claimed the division title because of their better conference record.

Bird again led the Celtics with a 21.2 scoring average and a 10.9 rebounding average. But Bird was not satisfied with the season. Only a championship would make things right.

Bird was named the NBA Rookie of the Year in 1979-80.

The First Championship

Bird and the Celtics reached the conference finals against the 76ers. Everyone expected a tough, 7-game series. But Philadelphia jumped out to a surprising 3 games to 1 lead and held a commanding lead in the final minutes of Game 5. It looked as though the 76ers would bounce the Celtics from the play-offs for the second year in a row.

Rallying behind the playmaking and shooting of Larry Bird, the Celtics won Game 5, 111-109. Another two-point win by the Celtics in Game 6 evened the series, setting the stage for a final showdown. Larry Bird hit a last-second jumper in Game 7, lifting the Celtics to a thrilling 91-90 win.

The championship series against the Houston Rockets proved to be anticlimactic as the Celtics won in six games, securing their fourteenth NBA title. Teammate Cedric Maxwell won the MVP award for the play-offs. But Larry Bird led the way with 21.9 points and 12.8 rebounds per game.

For the third consecutive year since Bird's arrival, the Celtics earned the league's best record in 1981-82, finishing 63-19. That included an impressive 18-game winning streak. But the pesky 76ers were right behind the Celtics again with a 58-24 record, and would prove to be a major obstacle in the play-offs.

Bird led the Celtics to an NBA championship in 1981.

Bird had another outstanding season. He finished with a team-high 22.9 scoring average while hauling down 10.9 rebounds per game. After defeating the Washington Bullets 4-1 in the opening round of the play-offs, Bird and the Celtics faced the 76ers.

Bird led the Celtics to an opening game rout at Boston, 121-81. But Philadelphia regrouped and stunned the Celtics 121-113 in Game 2. The 76ers took the next two games in Philadelphia, pushing Boston to the edge of elimination. But Bird led the way in games 5 and 6 as the Celtics won, forcing a seventh game in Boston. The home court was not an advantage, however, as the 76ers won 120-106.

By his own high standards, Bird did not have a great series. For the first time in his career, he did not lead the Celtics in post season scoring. But his rebounding and playmaking were never better, and he looked forward to leading the charge into the play-offs the following season.

Larry Bird had his best season to date in 1982-83, averaging a career-high 23.6 points per game. He also led the team with an 11.0 rebounding average. The Celtics ended the season with a 56-26 record. But the 76ers were the class of the league, finishing 65-17. For the first time since Bird joined the team, the Celtics finished a disappointing second.

Their dissatisfaction carried into the play-offs, where the Milwaukee Bucks swept them in four games. It was the first four-game sweep in team history, and Bird was bitter about it. "I'm gonna go back home this summer and work harder on basketball than I ever did before," he proclaimed.

Despite the disappointment in the play-offs, Larry Bird had established himself as one of the NBA's best. Since he joined the Celtics, he led them in scoring. He also led them to three first-place finishes and one NBA championship. And he had finished second in the MVP voting three years in a row. Still, Bird and his fans expected more. Nothing but another championship would do.

"That's why I play," Bird said. "I'm just greedy on them things—winning the championship. I've never felt that way any other time, no matter how big some other game was.

"I remember the first time we won," he added, "against Houston [in 1981]. We were way ahead at the end, and so I came out with three minutes left. My heart was pounding so on the bench, I thought it would jump out of my chest. You know what you feel? You just want everything to stop and to stay like that forever."

Becoming an MVP

The following season (1983-84) Bird responded like a champion. He led the Celtics to another first-place finish with a 62-20 record. He also had a career-high 24.2 scoring average, tops on the team. For his efforts, Bird was finally named the NBA's Most Valuable Player.

In the play-offs, Bird and the Celtics survived a seven-game series with the New York Knicks. Then they disposed of the Milwaukee Bucks in five games. That set up a championship showdown between the Celtics' Larry Bird and the Los Angeles Lakers' Magic Johnson. It was the first time Bird and Johnson faced each other in post season play since the 1979 NCAA championship. Everyone wondered: Who's better? Magic or Bird?

The Lakers surprised the Celtics in Game 1 at Boston, 115-109. Then the Celtics won Game 2 in overtime, 124-121. The series moved to Los Angeles where the Lakers won Game 3 in a rout, 137-104.

But just when it looked as though Magic Johnson would win the showdown, Larry Bird put his game into high gear. He led the Celtics to a 129-125 overtime win in Game 4. Then in Boston, Bird and the Celtics won Game 5, 121-103. The Lakers took Game 6 in Los Angeles, 119-108. But back in Boston, Bird and the Celtics stormed back to take the championship, 111-102. Bird was named the playoff MVP with an amazing 27.5 scoring average. He had gained his revenge over Magic Johnson.

Bird won his first MVP award in 1984.

Bird and Johnson never had the chance to get to know each other. Yet many said they didn't get along. "It was reported in the papers that they didn't like each other," said Magic's agent, Lon Rosen. "They started to believe it."

But after the play-offs, Bird and Johnson found themselves together, doing a Converse shoes TV commercial at Bird's home in French Lick. In no time, the ice had cracked. The two became good friends. They talked easily in Bird's living room, and rode three-wheelers around Bird's property.

"Before, we wouldn't say nothing," Johnson recalled. "We'd just be glaring at each other, wouldn't even shake each other's hands. But now we'll talk a little bit on the court: 'I got you that time,' 'What you doing on me?' 'You can't stop this,' 'You're too big to be out here.' Little stuff like that. It's fun."

In the 1984-85 season, Bird was at the peak of his career. He led the Celtics to another first-place finish (63-19) with a career-high 28.7 scoring average, second-highest in the league. He also established himself as one of the best three-point shooters in the game. For the second year in a row, Larry Bird won the league's MVP award.

In the play-offs, the Celtics rolled to the finals. But the Lakers were waiting for them, eager to gain revenge for last year's championship defeat. Bird and the Celtics looked unbeatable in the opening game, which they won 148-114. But the Lakers won Game 2, 109-102.

Returning to Los Angeles, the Lakers won Game 3, 136-111. But Bird and the Celtics rebounded to capture Game 4, 107-105.

The Lakers took the final game in Los Angeles, 120-111, setting up a Game 6 showdown in Boston. Though the Celtics hoped the home court would be an advantage, the Lakers controlled the game and won the championship, 111-100.

Throughout the play-offs, elbow and finger injuries hampered Bird. Still, he averaged a team-high 26 points and 9.1 rebounds per game. No one could deny that Bird and the Celtics were at the top of their game.

Building the Celtic Dynasty

Bird and the Celtics continued building their basketball dynasty the following season (1985-86). Though nagging back pain hampered Bird, he led the team in scoring (25.8) and rebounding (9.8). He also earned his third-consecutive MVP award, leading the Celtics to an incredible 67-15 season. It was good for another first-place finish in the Atlantic Division.

Bird and the Celtics met the Chicago Bulls and their high-flying star Michael Jordan in the first round of the play-offs. Jordan was dominant, but Bird and the Celtics had too much talent. They swept the Bulls in three games.

Bird won his third consecutive MVP award in 1986,
leading the Celtics to another NBA Championship.

The Celtics waltzed through the rest of the play-offs. They defeated the Atlanta Hawks 4 games to 1. Then they swept the Milwaukee Bucks in four games before finishing off the Houston Rockets 4 games to 2 to capture another NBA crown. Bird averaged a team-high 25.9 points and 9.3 rebounds per game and collected the play-off MVP trophy.

It seemed as though Bird and the Celtics would dominate the NBA forever. In the 1986-87 season, the Celtics won their division again with a 59-23 record. Bird led the way with a team-high 28.1 scoring average, but Magic Johnson ended Bird's three-year MVP reign.

In the play-offs, the Celtics easily defeated Chicago 3-0. But they looked tired in the next round against Milwaukee, barely eking out a 4-3 series win. Boston had a tough conference final series against the Detroit Pistons. They won the first two games in Boston, but then were blown out in games 3 and 4 in Detroit.

In Game 5 at Boston, the Pistons held the lead and the ball with five seconds remaining. It seemed certain that the Celtics would lose. If so, they would return to Detroit for Game 6 and face elimination.

But Larry Bird saved one more miracle for the Celtics. He stole Detroit guard Isiah Thomas' inbounds pass and threw it to teammate Dennis Johnson who sank the game-winning shot. Though Detroit won Game 6, Bird and the Celtics returned to Boston to win Game 7, setting up yet another championship meeting with Magic Johnson and the Los Angeles Lakers.

Celtic fans anticipated more miracles—and another championship—from Larry Bird. But the Lakers easily won the first two games in Los Angeles. Boston rallied at home 109-103 in Game 3. Then in Game 4, Bird made a three-pointer to put the Celtics up by two with seconds remaining. But after a Laker free throw, Magic Johnson hit a last-second hook shot that won the game 107-106.

Though the Celtics won Game 5, they had the near-impossible task of defeating the Lakers in the final two games at Los Angeles. The Lakers wasted little time capturing another NBA championship as they defeated the Celtics 106-93 in Game 6. Bird had once again led his team in playoff scoring (27.0) and rebounding (10.0). But fans sensed that the Celtic dynasty was coming to a close.

On the Decline

In 1987-88, the Celtics won their division again. But the result was misleading. Boston's 57-25 record was the only winning mark in the weak Atlantic Division. Still, Bird had his best scoring season ever with a 29.9 average, the third-best in the league.

The play-offs severely tested 32-year-old Bird and the Celtics. They defeated New York 3-1 in the opening round, then ran into a tough Atlanta Hawks team. Atlanta forced Boston into a Game 7 finale and took an early lead. But Bird exploded for 20 points in the fourth quarter and the Celtics barely won 118-116.

The seven-game battle against Atlanta proved costly. The Celtics looked tired against the Detroit Pistons. Detroit won two games in Boston en route to a 4-2 conference final win. Bird averaged 24.5 points per game in the play-offs, second to teammate Kevin McHale's 25.4 average. But many wondered if Bird could lead the Celtics back to glory in the coming season.

Fans got their answer as the 1988-89 season began. After only six games, Bird went out for the entire season with bone spurs in his heels. Without their MVP in the lineup, the Celtics finished a disappointing 42-40. The opening round of the play-offs proved to be a disaster, as the Pistons easily swept the Celtics in three games.

Bird missed most of the 1988-89 season with an injury.

That summer, Larry Bird returned to the basketball court after a 221 day absence. This time the game was at the Market Square Arena in Indianapolis, Indiana. It was an exhibition game called Larry's Game, organized by Bird to raise scholarship money for students in Indiana. On hand were NBA stars Michael Jordan of the Chicago Bulls and Dominique Wilkins of the Atlanta Hawks. Bird figured the game would be a good test for him.

Bird hit his first shot—a three-pointer—and went on to play 29 minutes. He scored 33 points as his team won 182-168. "I thought I'd be all right," he said afterward. "The last couple of weeks the workouts have been going really well. I wanted to use this as a test. I just wanted to get on the floor, make the passes, make the cuts. I wanted to see where my conditioning was."

Bird, now healthy, was eager to get back on track during the 1989-90 season. He returned to his usual spot as team scoring leader (24.3 average). But the Celtics (52-30) fell one game short of catching Philadelphia (53-29) for the division title.

Boston faced the New York Knickerbockers in the opening round of the play-offs. Bird led the way with a team-high 24.4 points per game as the Celtics won the first two games in Boston. But the Knicks won the last three games, including a 121-114 win at Boston in Game 5.

It seemed as though Bird and the Celtics were on the decline. They no longer dominated the league or the play-offs. And they were getting older.

Bird was determined to show that the better days were not behind him. In the 1990-91 season, he led the Celtics to a 29-5 start. But then disaster struck as Bird went down with a back injury that plagued him throughout the season. On long plane rides, he wore a back brace. When out of the lineup during a game, he laid in front of the Boston bench.

Bird played 60 games in the 82-game schedule, averaging a career-low 19.4 points per game, but still tops on the team. The Celtics won the division with a 56-26 record and faced the Indiana Pacers in the play-offs.

The Celtics beat the Pacers 3 games to 2, but then lost to Detroit 4-2 in the next round. Bird played in 10 of 11 playoff games, averaging only 17.1 points per game.

*As a three-time MVP, Bird has established himself
as one of the NBA's all-time great players.*

Back problems slowed him in 1991-92 as well. And Bird was forced to watch from the bench as the Celtics entered the play-offs. Despite his injury, Bird was named to the 1992 U.S. Olympic Basketball Team—a "dream" team composed of the N.B.A.'s finest players.

A Champion for All Time

Whether Larry Bird can come back one more time and attain his MVP status doesn't matter. Throughout his career, he has proven himself as a leader, a winner, and a champion. Without their most valuable player, the Celtics would not have enjoyed the success they achieved in the 1980s.

Bird downplays his individual achievements and reputation as one of the greatest basketball players of all time. "As far as that goes, it's enough for me that the [championship] flags are flying in Boston garden. When it's all over with, I'll just go off and be glad. At the end of every season, when you get up the next morning, you think: 'Hey, no bus to take today, no plane to catch tomorrow.' It's the greatest feeling—next to the championship."

Larry Bird's Address

You can write to Larry Bird at the following address:

Larry Bird
c/o The Boston Celtics
150 Causeway St.
Boston, MA 02114